Dad's Coming Home

Written by Diana Kimpton

Illustrated by Amanda Wood

Dad's coming home.

File Edit View Create Actions Help
Welcome Leela-inbox Hello Leela
NEW Reply Delete Folder COPY TOOLS
Leela Kumar
To
Leela
Subject
Hello Leela
Dear Leela
I am coming home today.
Love from
Dad

Hello Dad.
Where are you?
New
Honey
Bunnies

I am sitting in a taxi.

Where are you now, Dad?

I’m at the airport.
11:15
fly with us
TICKET

Where are you now?

I'm getting off the plane.

Where are you now, Dad?

KK331146

Where are you?

I’m walking up the road.